Princess Ponies

A Special Surprise

The Princess Ponies series

Princess Ponies

A Special Surprise

CHLOE RYDER

BLOOMSBURY

NEW YORK   LONDON   OXFORD   NEW DELHI   SYDNEY

First published in Great Britain in March 2014 by Bloomsbury Publishing Plc
Published in the United States of America in September 2015
by Bloomsbury Children's Books
www.bloomsbury.com

Bloomsbury is a registered trademark of Bloomsbury Publishing Plc

For information about permission to reproduce selections from this book, write to
Permissions, Bloomsbury Children's Books, 1385 Broadway, New York, New York 10018
Bloomsbury books may be purchased for business or promotional use. For information on
bulk purchases please contact Macmillan Corporate and Premium Sales Department at
specialmarkets@macmillan.com

Library of Congress Cataloging-in-Publication Data
Ryder, Chloe.
A special surprise / by Chloe Ryder.
pages   cm.   — (Princess ponies ; 7)
Summary: When a group of riding school ponies goes missing from the
human world, Pippa returns to the enchanted island of Chevalia, reuniting
with her horse friend, Princess Stardust, to solve the mystery.
ISBN 978-1-61963-565-4 (paperback) • ISBN 978-1-61963-566-1 (e-book)
[1. Ponies—Fiction. 2. Magic—Fiction. 3. Friendship—Fiction.] I. Title.
PZ7.R95898Sq 2015   [Fic]—dc23   2015010419

Typeset by Hewer Text UK Ltd, Edinburgh
Printed in China by Leo Paper Products, Heshan, Guangdong
4 6 8 10 9 7 5 3

With special thanks to Julie Sykes

Royal Family

King
Firestar

Prince
Jet

Prince
Comet

Prince
Storm

Chevalia

The castle was lit by torches. Their flickering flames cast long shadows as the girl and the pony rode into the courtyard. The girl wore a long striped T-shirt and leggings. Her hair was a thick mass of chestnut curls. The pony was snow-white, with a long mane and tail that brushed the floor. Her hooves were oiled and sparkled with gold dust. She carried her head proudly, her pink diamond-studded tiara glittering in the torchlight.

The castle walls were decorated with fresh flowers and ribbons. Music drifted through the air. The girl breathed slowly, resisting the urge to leap from the pony's back and dance. Ponies were packed around the edges of the court-yard. Their manes sparkled with jewels

and richly colored sashes hung around their necks. The girl and the pony walked toward the stage, where a pretty palomino with a golden coat and a tall, handsome copper-colored pony waited for them. Queen Moonshine and King Firestar smiled as the little white pony stopped. The girl slid from her back. Together they performed a low curtsy.

"Your Majesties," they murmured.

"Pippa MacDonald, Princess Stardust. The ponies of Chevalia salute you for finding the eight golden horseshoes and returning them to the Whispering Wall. Without you, we would have lost Chevalia forever."

The horseshoes glittered with Midsummer magic.

"To Pippa, to Princess Stardust," called Queen Moonshine.

"To Pippa, to Princess Stardust," echoed the ponies.

Pippa and Stardust curtsied to the ponies.

"To Chevalia," they answered.

Chapter 1

"Would you like some more chocolate cake, Pippa?" asked Mom.

Pippa looked at the cake. It was filled with buttercream and topped with chocolate sprinkles, and it tasted delicious. "I'm not sure. If I eat too much then I might be too heavy for Snowdrop to carry me over the jumps tomorrow."

Mom laughed. "Nonsense! Snowdrop's

a big strong horse. She could carry two of you."

Pippa smiled. "I'll have a little slice then, please. I need to keep my strength up. It was hard work jumping Snow-drop today. Did I tell you how we cleared the wall? Mrs. Woods said it was a perfect jump."

Miranda, Pippa's older sister, rolled her eyes. "Yes, but you've only told us about it six times."

"Have I? I'm really excited and nervous about the riding school competition tomorrow. It must be making me forgetful."

Pony-mad Pippa MacDonald was on a seaside vacation with her mom, Miranda, and younger brother Jack.

There were stables nearby and at the start of the vacation, Mom had secretly arranged for Pippa to have riding lessons there as a surprise. The stables had a pony called Snowdrop, named after a famous show pony. Pippa had a poster of the famous pony on her bedroom wall at home, so she was thrilled when she was given Snowdrop to ride.

Pippa had a secret too. On the first day of her vacation, two giant seahorses had whisked her away to Chevalia, a magical island where Royal Ponies reigned. Chevalia had been in danger. Pippa and her princess pony friend, Stardust, had saved the island by finding eight golden horseshoes. The horse-shoes had been stolen from an ancient wall in Stableside Castle by a wicked pony called Baroness Divine. Divine had escaped, but now the horseshoes were back in their rightful place and the Royal Ponies felt safe again.

Pippa finished eating her cake and then carried the plate to the sink. It was her turn to wash the dishes. As she played with the bubbles, she thought back to that magical day when she first met the seahorses. She'd had so many adventures in Chevalia. Pippa missed Stardust, especially today, as it was Stardust's birthday. Stardust would be celebrating with her family. Pippa wished she could be there too, but at least she had the riding school competition to look forward to.

After dinner, everyone crowded into

the living room to watch Pippa's favorite television show, a singing competition. But Pippa couldn't get into it. There was so much to do before tomorrow.

She went to her room to check if she had a clean shirt and jodhpurs to wear. Then she sat on the bedroom floor and polished her boots until she could see her reflection in them.

Tired but happy, Pippa rested her arms on the windowsill and stared out the window. The sinking sun spread a fiery red glow over the sea. Pippa breathed deeply, loving the smell of the salty sea air. It was so quiet. The only sound was the distant mewl of the herring gulls . . . and the strange rustling noise coming from the bushes under her window. Pippa stood very still. What was making that noise?

"Pippa, are you there?"

Pippa's heart jumped with disbelief. She recognized that voice.

"Stardust?" she called back.

"Yes, it's me." A pretty, white pony, wearing a tiara studded with sparkly pink diamonds, stepped from behind the bushes and appeared on the lawn. "Surprise!"

"Wait there! I'm coming down." Pippa shook with delight as she raced downstairs to the garden. What was Princess Stardust doing here, in the human world?

As Pippa tiptoed past the living room, she heard Mom, Miranda, and Jack laughing at something on the television. She went out the kitchen door and hurried to the back of the house.

"Stardust," Pippa said as she wrapped her arms around her best pony friend's neck and hugged her. "Happy birthday. What are you doing here? Aren't you having a party in Chevalia?"

Stardust blew softly in Pippa's wavy brown hair.

"I've missed you," she said. "You're my best friend forever. I knew you wouldn't forget my birthday."

"Who forgot?" asked Pippa.

"Everyone!" Stardust turned pink. "It was just like any other normal day. Last year my entire family surprised me at breakfast by singing 'Happy Birthday,' but this year, nothing. No cards, no presents, no cake nor candles."

"Oh!" Pippa was speechless. Even though she'd been taught not to expect cards and presents, her family and friends always gave her things on her birthday. She knew she'd be as disappointed as Stardust if they didn't. "Maybe everyone was in a rush. Perhaps they'll make a fuss over you at dinner?"

Stardust shook her head.

"Mom and Dad went out for the day. They won't be back until late. I was so upset that after school I went down to the beach. Cloud was flying past. When she saw me, I jumped up on my hind hooves and rubbed noses with her, giving me wings so that I could fly wherever I wanted to. I flew straight here to see you."

Cloud was one of Stardust's sisters. She had special magical powers that enabled her to fly. She used them to rescue ponies in distress and then take them to Chevalia. Any horse that rubbed noses with Cloud grew wings too, but the moment their hooves touched the ground the wings disappeared.

"Cloud gave you a present then," said Pippa.

"I suppose so." Stardust looked shocked. "But I've wasted the present by touching the ground. Now we can't go flying together."

"That would have been fun, but it's almost my bedtime," said Pippa.

"Bedtime? It was afternoon when I left Chevalia."

"Well, it's bedtime here," said Pippa. "Remember that Chevalia is in a magic time bubble. When I came to the island, no time passed in my world while I was there, so I wasn't missed by my family. Perhaps it's the same for you?"

"Perhaps. Not that my friends and family would miss me anyway. I'm just the foal. They've got far more important things to do than worry about me, or celebrate my birthday." Stardust's brown eyes were bright with unshed tears.

"That's not true," said Pippa, stroking her neck. "I'll celebrate your birthday with you if you like."

Stardust smiled.

"Really? Let's have a birthday sleepover then. We could decorate your bedroom and have a midnight feast of honey-covered oats and sugar-dipped carrots."

Pippa blushed.

"That would be fun," she said carefully. "But we can't. The vacation cottage is too tiny. There isn't room for you, me, and Miranda in our shared bedroom. You can stay the night, though." She scrunched her eyes shut while she thought about where Stardust could sleep. "I'll take you to the riding school. They've got an empty stall."

"A *riding school*! How exciting! I'd love that. Thanks, Pippa. You really are my best friend."

Pippa looked at her watch. "It's not

far. I'll need to ask Mom if I can go for a walk first." She ran inside and was back a minute later. "I have to be back in half an hour."

"Would you like to ride me?" asked Stardust. "It'll be much quicker."

"Yes please." Pippa wrapped her hands in Stardust's soft, white mane then vaulted onto her back. "I've missed you," she said, stroking Stardust's neck.

"I've missed you too," Stardust whinnied happily as she trotted along the garden path.

Chapter 2

Pippa guided Stardust around the edge of a ripening barley field, speckled with poppies.

"This reminds me of the Grasslands back in Chevalia," said Stardust.

The golden barley rustled as they trotted by. Butterflies and bees fluttered around the red poppies. Hidden crickets chirped loudly, falling silent as Pippa and Stardust drew near.

"Are you sure this is the right way?" asked Stardust. "All I can see is more fields."

"It's not far now," said Pippa. "One more field and we're there. I can walk if you like."

"No," said Stardust quickly. "I love being ridden. My best pony friend, Blossom, is too busy to play with me. She's training for the Annual Autumn Marathon. Honey's no fun either. She's been in a bad mood since Canter's banned us from wearing hoof polish at school. I don't know why they're being so strict about it. All the teachers wear it. It's just not fair. Oh, and did I tell you that Comet's writing a book? It's about the missing horseshoes. He's driving me crazy, asking me questions about how we found them. And you'll never guess what I saw the other day." Stardust didn't wait for Pippa to reply. "Crystal and Trojan were rubbing noses behind the haunted house at the fairground. *Eeeww!* Luckily I've got Cinders to keep me company. She boards at Canter's now. She's much nicer since Baroness Divine ran away."

"Do you think Divine will come back?" asked Pippa.

"I hope not." Stardust shivered. "But at least everyone knows how wicked she is. Poor Cinders—it must have been such a shock to learn that her own mother had stolen the horseshoes."

They walked in silence until they

reached the end of the field. Pippa guided Stardust onto a narrow lane with high banks. "There are the stables." Pippa pointed to a driveway at the end of the lane where a wooden sign read *Barley Field Stables*.

"We can't get in," said Stardust, stopping at a five-bar gate that was chained and locked.

"I know the code." Pippa leaned down to the lock and spun the numbers on the dial. It clicked open and she pushed the gate wide.

Stardust whinnied in surprise.

"How did you do that? Did you use magic?"

"No," chuckled Pippa. "It's something called technology."

The wooden stable block consisted

of eight stalls arranged in an L-shape behind the indoor school. Stardust stopped dead.

"Is that it?"

"Yes," said Pippa, sliding from her back. "Only six ponies are in tonight. The others are out in the fields, so you've got two whole stalls to choose from."

"I can't sleep here," said Stardust. Her nose wrinkled as she peered into one of the empty stalls. "Where's the bed? Why is the straw on the floor and not under a blanket? There aren't any pictures on the walls, and anyone can look at me over the door. This is no place for a princess!"

"*Shhh*," said Pippa. She glanced around but it was too late. Stardust had woken the other ponies.

"What's all that noise?" grumbled a chestnut pony named Rose.

"Is it a new pony? I'm Sunflower. Pleased to meet you," called a pretty palomino.

"Hello, Pippa," called Snowdrop. "Who's your friend?"

Pippa felt as if her head were spinning. "You can talk? Why haven't you spoken to me before?"

"We talk to you all the time," said Snowdrop. "We didn't think you could understand us."

"This is the first time I've heard you." Pippa looked, thinking. "Maybe I can hear you now because of Stardust." The pony's tiara was sparkling more brightly than usual. "It must be princess pony magic at work."

Stardust stepped forward and curtsied to Snowdrop. "I'm Princess Stardust of Chevalia—and you are?"

Snowdrop started to answer, but a tall gray pony stuck her nose out of a nearby stall.

"Welcome, Princess Stardust. I'm Petunia of Barley Field Stables. I'm in charge here."

"No, you're not," the other ponies neighed.

Petunia ignored them. "The stall next to mine is free. Why don't you sleep there?"

A hopeful look crossed Stardust's face. She trotted to the other empty stall and stared over the door.

"It's worse than the other one. I'll get my hooves dirty if I sleep in there."

"Ooh, isn't she *la-di-dah!*" said Hawthorn. A strand of hay hung from between his lips, and there were knots in his mane and tail.

BRAMBLE

PETUNIA

"Of course she can't sleep in there," agreed Rose, in a voice that meant exactly the opposite. "After all, she is a *princess*."

"Too right." Bramble stamped his hoof. "Someone find the princess a bed."

"Thank you," said Stardust, not realizing that the ponies were making fun of her.

"Wait," called Rose. "She can sleep in the stable only if she's taking part in the competition tomorrow. That's why Mrs. Woods brought us in for the night. The ponies not being ridden have to sleep in the field."

"I'd love to be in the competition. Pippa and I are great together. Did she tell you how . . ."

"Pippa's my girl," interrupted Snowdrop. "We've been practicing all week for the competition. We're the only pony and rider that can jump the wall without knocking it down."

"They still might let me enter," said Stardust quickly. "Pippa and I have been riding together for ages. Has she told you about our adventures in Chevalia?"

Petunia pricked up her ears. "Chevalia? Is that the stable down the road where the show ponies live?"

"Chevalia is the best place in the whole world," said Stardust. Her eyes misted over. "It's a magical island in the middle of the sea, filled with ponies."

Snowdrop stomped a hoof. "Pippa's

my girl," she repeated. "She can't change ponies now."

Pippa had to fight the urge to put her hands over her ears so she didn't have to listen to the squabbling. Taking a deep breath she spoke in a calm, clear voice.

"Stardust can't take part in the competition tomorrow because she has to go home. But she really needs a bed for the night, and it's her birthday. Please can she sleep in one of the spare stalls? I promise I'll come and get her first thing tomorrow morning before Mrs. Woods arrives."

Snowdrop thought about it.

"Well, if it's her birthday then of course she can stay for a night. We can't let her sleep in the field. Why don't you sleep here in the stall next to me?"

Stardust hesitated. "I've never been on a sleepover before. I haven't slept in a stall either."

"Really? It'll be fine, I promise," said Snowdrop kindly. "Go on in and make yourself comfortable. When you're settled, you can tell us all about Chevalia."

"I'd love to." Stardust nuzzled her nose in Pippa's wavy brown hair. "You'll come back for me early tomorrow?"

"I promise," said Pippa. "Good night, Stardust. Don't stay up all night talking."

"I won't. Well, I might," she snorted.

As Pippa hurried down the drive, she could hear Stardust's voice.

"When I was a little foal, I desperately wanted a pet girl. Every stone on my bedroom wall at Stableside Castle is covered with pictures of them . . ."

Pippa smiled as she ran home through the fields.

Chapter 3

The following morning Pippa wasn't sure if she'd dreamed that Stardust had visited her. As she took her new turquoise polo shirt from its hanger and picked up her jodhpurs, she noticed a long, white hair on the dark carpet. Pippa held it up. It was a strand of mane, much longer than Snow-drop's, and it sparkled. Pippa's heart raced with excitement as she pulled on her jodhpurs. Stardust really was here in her world! In the other bed, Miranda was still asleep. Pippa tiptoed out of her room and was halfway down the stairs when she had a thought. She crept back to the bedroom for the tiara that Stardust had given her to say thank you for her help in rescuing Chevalia's eight precious horseshoes. She pushed it into her wavy hair and adjusted it so that it sat on top of her head.

After a quick breakfast of cereal and toast, Pippa pulled on her riding boots and left the cottage. She ran all the way to the stables and skipped through the unlocked gate. It was very quiet as Pippa approached the stable block. There was no rustle of hooves on straw or the swish of a tail. Pippa grinned to herself.

"I bet they were up all night listening to Stardust's stories. They'd better not be too tired to take part in the competition."

Pippa entered the yard and stopped dead. Her mouth opened but the words were stuck in her throat.

"Stardust, Snowdrop, Sunflower, Rose . . ." Pippa rushed from stall to stall—they were all empty. The ponies were gone.

"Hello, Pippa dear. You're early this morning. I haven't cleaned out the stalls yet, but you can tie Snowdrop up in the yard to groom her if you like," said Mrs. Woods as she walked into the yard.

Pippa turned around. Her riding teacher was dressed in her old clothes—a faded top, a torn pair of jeans, and green boots. Her hair was tied back in a neat ponytail.

"The p-p-ponies. They're gone," Pippa stuttered.

"Gone?" The color drained from Mrs. Woods's face. She rushed around, looking into every stall. Then she pinched herself hard.

"Ouch! It's not a nightmare then. This is terrible. Someone's stolen my ponies."

Mrs. Woods's hands shook as she pulled her cell phone from her pocket and called the police. Pippa was shaking too. It was bad enough that the riding school ponies were missing but worse still for Stardust, who didn't even belong there.

"Yes," said Mrs. Woods, speaking into her cell phone. "I was the last person to leave and I definitely locked the gate."

Pippa froze. Guilt flooded through her. Mrs. Woods hadn't been the last person at the stables last night. She had. Had she locked the gate as she left? To her horror, Pippa couldn't remember.

Mrs. Woods ended her call. She patted Pippa on the arm.

"I'm so sorry but I'll have to cancel the competition. I'll call the parents of the other children and tell them in a moment, but first I want to look in the stall next to Snowdrop's again."

Pippa followed Mrs. Woods into the stall where Stardust had spent the night. Her face burned when Mrs. Woods said, "This stall was empty, only it looks like a pony has slept here." She laughed a little. "How silly of me! I guess I didn't clean the stall out properly after it was last used."

Pippa stared at the straw scattered over the floor. Stardust must have had a restless night, or maybe there'd been a struggle when the horse thieves captured her. Pippa shivered. Poor Stardust! She must have been so frightened.

"You might as well go home, Pippa," said Mrs. Woods kindly. "I'll call you if I hear anything. I'm very sorry. I hope it hasn't spoiled your vacation."

"Could I look around before I go?" asked Pippa. "In case there are any clues?"

Mrs. Woods hesitated. "You can look, but please don't touch anything. If you find any clues, let me know. The police will need to see them too."

"Okay," said Pippa.

Mrs. Woods walked to her office, and Pippa began to look around the yard. Apart from Stardust's rumpled stall, it was spotless. There wasn't anything out of the ordinary at all. Except . . . Pippa crouched down to look at a series of black marks that crossed the yard and ended at the stable block. Her eyes widened in disbelief. "It can't be." She stared at the black marks again. They were a series of tiny horseshoes. "That's impossible!" Pippa traced a finger around one of the hoofprints. It made a black mark on her finger—as black as the rock from the volcano on Chevalia, where the Night Mares had once lived under the rule of Baroness Divine. Pippa's finger tingled unpleasantly.

"Dark magic," said Pippa. She now had a very good idea who had stolen the ponies—wicked Divine. She also knew where to start looking for them—Chevalia. "Chevalia, here I come," said Pippa as she ran down the drive.

Pippa ran all the way down the winding path that led to Horseshoe Cove. She burst out onto the beach. Her riding boots sank into the powdery sand, and she reached the surf line sweaty and panting. Pippa stood with her hands shielding her eyes from the sparkling water, while she got her breath back.

"Triton, Rosella." Pippa shouted the names of the giant seahorses that had first carried her to Chevalia. "Triton, Rosella, I need your help."

She touched her tiara and felt the magic of Chevalia fizz through her fingers. Seconds later there was a whooshing noise. The sea reared up in a huge wave, in the shape of the head and

forelegs of a galloping horse. Pippa felt relieved as two giant seahorses exploded through the motionless wave and stared expectantly at her.

Chapter 4

"Triton, Rosella." Pippa reached out to stroke Rosella's pale pink face and Triton's freckled green one. "Something terrible has happened."

Pippa quickly told her story. She was coming to the end when she heard the muffled thud of hooves on the sand. She turned around to see a white pony galloping along the sand.

"Stardust!" The relief made her heart soar. "You're safe."

Stardust blew through her nose at Pippa. "Yes, because I didn't sleep in that horrible stall. I was halfway through my story of how we saved Chevalia when I realized that Snowdrop was snoring. Snoring!" Stardust repeated in disgust. "She wasn't the only one. All the ponies had fallen asleep. I tried to get comfortable, but the straw was scratchy, the ground too hard, and there was a funny smell." Stardust gave a dainty shudder. "I need my beauty sleep or I get saddlebags under my eyes. That's when I decided to sleep outside in the field. It was a bit like the time I went camping with Honey and Comet, except that the horseflies here aren't as friendly as the ones back home."

"Where are the riding school ponies?" Pippa interrupted.

Stardust's eyes opened wide with fear. "I was just getting to that part. Divine took them. I'm sure it was her. I was woken by the sound of hooves. Then I heard a cackling laugh. There was a lot of gray smoke and a very bad smell.

It made my eyes water. When the smoke cleared, the riding school ponies were gone."

Pippa felt scared. "But what would Divine want with a stable full of ponies?"

"Maybe she's lonely," said Stardust.

"Perhaps she needs new ponies to do her dirty work, since the volcano ponies discovered how mean she was," suggested Triton.

"I knew it was Divine," said Pippa. "I'm going back to Chevalia to find the ponies. That's if you'll take me there?" Pippa looked at Triton and Rosella.

"Of course we will."

"What about me?" Stardust wailed. "I lost the wings that Cloud gave me when I landed here. How am I going to get home?"

Triton put his nose inside his pouch and brought out a small blue bottle that glowed mysteriously.

"Can you keep a secret?" he asked.

Pippa and Stardust nodded.

"This bottle contains a powerful growing potion. It's an ancient formula that was invented by Nightingale."

"Nightingale, the horse who made the golden horseshoes?" asked Pippa.

Triton nodded.

"Yes, she's the pony who changed the volcanic rock into the island of Chevalia," added Rosella. "Long ago my seahorse ancestors took messages from Chevalia to the human world. We're still needed to take messages back and forth between the worlds. The work can be dangerous, especially if the weather is stormy. Every pair of sea-horses has a supply of magic potions, just in case we need help."

Pippa's eyes widened. She thought she knew everything about Chevalia, but it still continued to surprise her.

Triton flicked up a shell from the seabed with his tail. He sprinkled two drops of the potion on it. The lilac-colored drops sparkled and the shell began to grow until it was twice the size of Stardust.

"Climb aboard, Stardust," called Rosella.

Stardust trotted through the surf,

splashing water everywhere as she jumped onto the shell.

"Ready, Pippa?" asked Triton in a kind voice.

Pippa nodded and then scrambled onto Triton's back. She just had time to grab hold of one of his spines as the seahorse took off. Even though Pippa was worried about the riding school ponies, she couldn't help enjoying the journey to Chevalia. Riding a seahorse was as much fun as riding a pony. After a while Pippa saw a smudge on the horizon. The smudge grew larger and turned into an island fringed with soft, white sand. Pippa's heart swelled with excitement. It was good to be back in Chevalia.

Triton and Rosella stopped in the shallows. Triton gently tipped Pippa into the clear blue water, and Rosella helped Stardust down from the shell.

"Thank you," said Pippa.

Triton pulled another bottle, green this time, out of his pouch and sprinkled the shell with two drops of liquid. In a flash of green light it returned to its normal size and sank into the sand. Both of the seahorses dipped their heads in farewell.

"Good luck," they called as they swam out to sea.

Pippa and Stardust splashed onto the beach.

"Get on my back," said Stardust. "It'll be quicker if you ride me."

Pippa twisted a handful of mane around her hands and held on to Stardust with her knees. The princess pony galloped through the Wild Forest, across the grassy Fields and up the twisty path to Stableside Castle.

The castle, with its eight tall towers, was even bigger than Pippa had remembered. They clattered across the wooden drawbridge and rode into the courtyard. Seeing the eight golden horseshoes hanging on the ancient wall, Pippa swelled with pride. Stardust stopped sharply and Pippa nearly flew over her head.

"Mom, Dad! What are you doing here? I thought you'd gone out."

A dainty palomino with a golden coat and pure white mane and tail and a tall, handsome copper-colored pony were standing underneath a horseshoe-shaped glitter ball. Their eyes were sad and their shoulders hunched. The courtyard was decorated with fresh flowers, colored ribbon rosettes, and streamers.

"Your Majesties." Pippa slipped off Stardust's back and bowed to Queen Moonshine and King Firestar.

"Pippa MacDonald! Welcome back to Chevalia. And Stardust . . ." Relief flooded the King's face. "We were starting to worry about you."

"You were worried about me?" Stardust looked confused.

"The guests are arriving for your surprise birthday party," said the queen. She straightened a lock of Stardust's mane. "Your father and I pretended to go out so that you wouldn't find out about the party. But when you ran off so quickly after school, we thought we might have been too convincing. Were you upset when we didn't make a fuss over you?"

Stardust turned redder than a platter of strawberries. "I was a bit."

Princess Crystal trotted into the courtyard.

"There you are! And Pippa too!" She turned to the princes and princesses who were following her. "See, I told you there was nothing to worry about. Your sister hadn't run away. She'd gone to fetch her best friend, Pippa. I don't know what you've been doing. You look like you've been dragged through a haystack sideways. Trot along and tidy up before the guests start to arrive."

"I can't," said Stardust. "I'm sorry to spoil my surprise birthday party, but I've got something more important to do first. Some ponies have gone missing from Pippa's world. I think Divine might have something to do with it."

"Divine!" The ponies gasped with surprise and horror.

As Stardust told her family all about the missing ponies, Pippa couldn't help feeling impressed. When she'd first met her, Stardust would have hated to miss her own birthday party. She sounded very grown-up as she explained that she couldn't enjoy herself until all the riding school ponies had been found.

As Stardust finished speaking, her older brother Jet said, "Divine's been spotted recently near the haunted castle ruins in the Horseshoe Hills. Some ponies say that she's living there."

"Really?" Comet was annoyed. He scowled at Jet through his round glasses. "Why didn't you tell me before? You know how much I'd like to interview her for the book I'm writing."

Jet shrugged. "There isn't any proof, and I don't spread pony tales."

Princess Crystal snorted loudly. "The only interview Divine will be giving, once she's captured, is to the Royal Court. She still has to answer for stealing the horseshoes."

"If Divine's been seen near the

ruins, then we should start there," said Stardust.

A haunted castle! Pippa shivered. Why couldn't Divine have chosen somewhere less scary to hide?

Bravely she said, "The spooky ruins of a castle sound just like the sort of place that Divine would make her new home. Let's go there now."

"You can't go on your own. We'd better come with you," Crystal said bossily.

"We found the missing horseshoes without any help, and it'll be quicker if Pippa and I go alone," said Stardust.

Princess Crystal opened her mouth to argue but Queen Moonshine was already speaking. "Stardust, Pippa, go. Go and rescue those poor riding school ponies."

Chapter 5

Racing across the island on Stardust's back was so much fun that Pippa almost forgot where they were going. She held on tightly, leaning forward to shout encouragement in Stardust's ear. The wind whipped through her wavy hair and blew it over her face. Pippa gave up trying to push it out of her eyes and put her trust in Stardust as they galloped up the craggy paths through the Horseshoe Hills. The higher they climbed, the fiercer the wind blew and the more rugged the path became. Stardust slowed to a trot and then to a walk. She moved forward one hoof at a time. Pippa looked down and immediately wished she hadn't. They were traveling along a ridge with a river hurtling through the gorge below. Pippa's stomach lurched and she tightened her grip on Stardust's mane. "Look up," she reminded herself, but even though she didn't want to look down at the jagged cliff face, it was hard to look away.

"Are you okay?" called Stardust. She twisted her neck to look at Pippa.

"Yes," replied Pippa through gritted

teeth. She wished Stardust would concentrate on the path and not on her.

"I think we're almost there." Loose stones rattled under Stardust's hooves. Her neck was lathered with sweat and she was breathing heavily. Pippa knew she should offer to walk, but she didn't dare. The path was too narrow to dismount safely.

Stardust's steps became slower until at last the path widened. Spiky-leaved plants with small flowers clung to the rocks. The path dipped then rose. They came over the hill and into a grassy hollow. Stardust stopped dead.

"Oh!" gasped Pippa. She slid from Stardust's back and stood with her hand around her neck. "It's really creepy."

This castle was nothing like Stable-side. It was smaller and mostly in ruins. Ivy grew everywhere, blackening the outside with its thick woody stems and dark green leaves. The towers were crumbling and through the run-down walls Pippa saw a dismal round room with plants growing through the floor. The massive front door was covered in cobwebs. Pippa shivered and clamped her lips together to stop her teeth from chattering. A thin curl of smoke rose from the back of the building.

"Someone's home," said Pippa. Her arms broke out in goose bumps. Taking a deep breath she added, "Shall we find out who?"

Stardust nodded. Her eyes looked

round and her nostrils flared. On the tips of toes and hooves, Pippa and Stardust crept closer and around the side of the building. The ivy grew thicker here, covering the window slits. Pippa tore it aside. Dirt flicked in her face and something pricked her finger.

"Ouch," she said as she sucked it to stop it from stinging. This time she was more careful as she ripped the ivy from the walls. The first few rooms they looked into were empty except for dust and cobwebs that hung from the ceiling like thick, gray curtains. They found the kitchen, a vast room with a huge stone fireplace. There was a stone feeding trough draped with a few rotting carrots and another for water.

"*Eeew!* I wouldn't drink from that," said Stardust.

They continued on until they reached almost the end of the building. Pippa had a hard time pulling the ivy from the window slit. She was about to give up and go around to the back of the castle when she heard a noise. She put a finger to her lips to warn Stardust. With extra care Pippa pulled back the ivy. A familiar voice drifted through the air.

"Volcanica was mine . . . stole it from me . . . if I can't have it . . . so you see . . . pony world . . . here . . . mine . . . all MINE!"

Pippa stared at Stardust. "She's power crazy. Listen to her, mumbling to herself."

"What did she mean by 'pony world'?" asked Stardust.

"I don't know." Pippa pushed her face against the window opening. It was dark inside and it took her eyes a while to adjust. A sour smell drifted toward her. Pippa's throat constricted. She swallowed hard, choking back the cough that threatened to give her away.

"Can you see anything?" hissed Stardust.

Pippa's eyes swept the room. It was set up as a laboratory. A complicated piece of glassware, supported with a metal stand and clamps, sat over a small fire. A vile yellow liquid bubbled inside a round-bottomed flask. Clouds of smoke billowed from the opening and over to the window slit. Pippa turned her head away, took a deep breath of fresh air, then looked through the window again. Her pulse raced as she spotted Divine, dressed in her long dark cloak, leaning over a sturdy oak table. Her lips were moving and suddenly Pippa realized she wasn't talking to herself after all.

"No!" she gasped. "It can't be."

"What?" asked Stardust, bumping Pippa as she tried to look.

Pippa stepped to the side. "Mini ponies," she breathed. "On the table. They look like . . . but that's impossible." She rubbed her eyes with her fists then stared again. "Oh no! It's worse than we thought. That tiny, white pony is Snow- drop." She stared at the ponies. They were the same size as the animals in her brother's farmyard set. "Divine has shrunk all the riding school ponies."

"No way!" exclaimed Stardust. She stared into the room. Divine stood over the table. Her eyes gleamed with madness as she talked to the tiny ponies huddled together next to a battered satchel. "How did she get to the human world? And why would she steal the riding school ponies? What's she up to?"

Pippa pulled away from the window. Stardust followed, and they crept back to the front of the house where Divine wouldn't hear them.

"Maybe she followed you," Pippa said.

"But she'd have needed wings to fly after me," said Stardust thoughtfully. "What do we do now?"

"Confront her," Pippa said boldly, even though she was trembling at the idea.

A fearful look crossed Stardust's face, then she drew herself up and said bravely, "Let's do it."

The front door was locked. In frustration Pippa shoved her shoulder against it, but it didn't even budge.

"We'll have to climb through a window," she said.

Pippa found one with loose bricks around the opening. With Stardust's help she pried the bricks away until the window was large enough for her to climb through. Pippa was trembling as she ran along the dusty corridor to open the front door for Stardust.

"Thanks," whispered Stardust as the door swung open.

They crept through the castle, stepping carefully to avoid the rubble littering the floor. A rat scurried across their path and Stardust reared up.

"*Eeek!* I hate rats," she snorted.

"I don't like spiders," Pippa said sympathetically.

"Don't look up then," said Stardust.

Pippa couldn't help it and only just stopped herself from screaming when she saw an enormous spider dangling from the ceiling. Her heart was thumping so loudly she was sure Divine would hear it. Pippa clutched her hands to her chest to muffle the rapid thud. When they arrived outside Divine's makeshift laboratory, Pippa paused.

"Ready?" she asked.

Stardust nodded. Pippa pushed on the handle and the door creaked open. Divine was still hunched over the table. She looked up, startled.

"You!" she screeched at Pippa and Stardust. "Haven't you interfered enough? This is my castle. Get out!"

"Hello, Divine," said Pippa. "We're not leaving until we get the riding school ponies back."

"They're mine," said Divine, putting a hoof around them. "And soon I'll have more!"

"They're not yours." Pippa stepped forward. "You took them from my world."

"How did you get there? Did you follow me?" asked Stardust.

An evil smile spread across Divine's face. "Of course I followed you. Silly little foal. I knew if I waited long enough you'd weaken and need to visit your *pet* girl."

"But how could you fly? Cloud would never have given you wings."

Divine threw back her head and cackled with laughter. "Have you forgotten my ancestors? I'm a direct descendant of Nightingale. She was a genius. I took her scrolls and note-books from Volcanica. I know all her secrets. I can make flying potions, growing lotions, shrink drinks. Her science and magic make me the most powerful pony on Chevalia! There's nothing I can't do now!"

"So you shrank the riding school ponies!" Pippa stared at the six tiny horses cowering on the table.

Divine gave a half bow. "I *saved* the riding school ponies. They didn't want to stay in the human world, performing tricks for silly little girls and boys, so I freed them from their miserable lives. These ponies love me. They are the start of my new empire. I'm going back to the human world to collect more ponies."

"That's not true," Pippa said angrily.

"The ponies love the riding school! Snowdrop's always pleased to see me. She wouldn't jump so well if she hated doing it. And Mrs. Woods really cares for her ponies."

"Enough!" Divine snatched up the satchel and hung it around her neck. With one quick move she flipped the end of the table with her nose. As the table tilted, the six tiny riding school ponies slid toward her. Divine opened the satchel wider and caught the helpless ponies as they slid off the end.

"Pippa!" squeaked Snowdrop in alarm. "Help us. We want to go home."

Pippa lunged for the satchel. "Give me that." But Divine reared up, forcing Pippa to jump back.

"Good-bye, interfering girl, good-bye *Princess*. Let's not meet again." With an evil cackle Divine ran through the door.

"Quick!" shouted Pippa, racing after her. "We can't let her get away."

Chapter 6

Divine fled along a short corridor and burst through a door at the back of the castle. Once outside she kicked it shut with her back hooves. Pippa stuck her foot in the doorway just in time to stop it from closing.

"Hop on," cried Stardust.

Pippa jumped onto Stardust's back, and the pony took off. The narrow path climbed steeply up the mountain. Pippa felt a rush of fear and excitement as they hurtled over the rugged ground.

"She's heading for the ridge," shouted Stardust. "We've got to stop her before she crosses over or we won't see which path she takes."

Pippa's mind whizzed like a blender. There wasn't enough room to overtake Divine, so how else could they stop her? Soon the path ahead forked. One way led up and the other down. In a low voice Pippa called to Stardust, "How can we make Divine choose the path down to the beach?"

"Like this," Stardust whispered back. "Hey, Pippa," she shouted loud enough for Divine to hear this time. "Which path do you think Divine will take?"

"Up," Pippa yelled back. "She'll definitely go up."

Ahead of them Divine positioned herself as if to take the path going up. Pippa held her breath. At the very last moment Divine swung left and took the other path. Stardust had anticipated that Divine would do the opposite of what Pippa had said and was already committed to going down. As she galloped after Divine, the gap between them slowly closed.

The path to the beach was even more treacherous than the route up to the spooky castle. Pippa clung on to Stardust with her hands and legs and kept her eyes fixed on the pony's white ears. Stones spun from Stardust's hooves and once she skidded. Pippa gasped and shot forward. For a few bumpy strides she clung to Stardust's neck until she was able to push herself back. A trickle of sweat rolled from her hairline and down her face. It tickled but Pippa was too scared to wipe it away.

She could hear the faint *shush* of the waves on the beach and smell the salty sea air. The path twisted and turned, then opened into a small cove with a sandy, white beach. Ahead of them, the sea sparkled in the sunlight. Behind, the cliffs rose up to the Horseshoe Hills. Divine pulled up at the water's edge. Her eyes were wild. "Think you're clever, do you, tricking me like that? Well, the joke's on you." She dropped her head and caught the satchel as it fell over her neck. She flipped it open and held it over the water. "If I can't have the riding school ponies, then no one can."

"Stop," said Stardust. She pawed at the sand. "Please don't hurt them. The ponies haven't done anything wrong."

Pippa slid from Stardust's back. The sea breeze caught her hair and dragged it over her face.

"Stay back, silly girl." Divine swung the satchel. "One hoof closer and I'll drop them."

Pippa pushed her curls out of her eyes. Her fingers brushed against something solid. The tiara. She'd forgotten she was wearing it. It reminded her of Triton and Rosella.

"I wish they were here now," she murmured.

Divine swung the satchel higher. Pippa held her breath. She thought she could hear the tiny riding school ponies whinnying in fear. If Divine wasn't careful, they could fall out into the sea. Without thinking, Pippa stepped closer to the water. A wave washed over her sandals. She felt her toes tingle with magic.

"Stay back!" screamed Divine. She swung the satchel even higher and then let go.

Pippa watched in horror as the satchel spun in the air. She leaped forward and ran into the sea. Everything seemed to slow—the spinning satchel, her legs as they splashed through the surf. She jumped up, her arms extended to catch the satchel, but she wasn't close enough. From the corner of her eye she saw Divine's triumphant smile as the satchel plummeted. Pippa braced herself for the splash, and when it came she was shocked at how loud it was. The sea looked like it had been hit by a mini whirlpool. She'd never find the riding school horses now. Then she gasped. Triton and Rosella burst through a wave. Rosella lunged and caught the satchel in her mouth.

"Great catch!" Pippa cheered.

Rosella's face darkened. "What's in here?"

"They're ponies from my riding school," said Pippa. "Divine has shrunk them with a magic potion. And she's going back to my world to steal more ponies."

Rosella nosed open the satchel. The ponies snorted and the satchel bulged as they backed into a corner.

"It's all right," said Rosella gently. "You're safe now."

"Mine," shrieked Divine. "Give me that. The ponies are mine."

Divine dived for the satchel, but Rosella swam out of her way.

"How dare you! The seahorses always

answered to my ancestor Nightingale, and you must obey me too."

"Never," said Triton. "Our ancestors were happy to serve Nightingale. She was a great scientist-magician. She was also kindhearted and used her magic and talents to help ponies in need by creating Chevalia."

"She would be ashamed of you," added Rosella.

Triton reached into his pouch and pulled out the blue bottle of growing potion. Skillfully, he sprinkled twelve drops over the satchel. The liquid sparkled and turned to lilac as it landed in the bag. There was a startled neigh and then two hooves burst out of the satchel. Snowdrop shook herself as she jumped out of the bag and landed in the surf. She was followed by Sunflower, Rose, Bramble, and Hawthorn. The ponies flattened their ears and hunched their shoulders as they stared nervously around.

"About time too," said Petunia, the last out of the bag. "It was hot and smelly in there."

Rosella guided the ponies through the surf and onto the beach. Snowdrop hung back and went to Pippa, who was knee-deep in the sea. She nuzzled her nose against Pippa's neck.

"Thank you, Pippa, lover of ponies. I knew you'd rescue us."

"Stardust, Rosella, and Triton helped too," said Pippa, including her friends with a wave of her hand.

"Ponies, wait! She's no friend of yours," Divine screeched. "Come with me and you'll never have to be ridden by silly little girls."

"I like being ridden," said Snowdrop. "It's fun."

"I do too."

"And me too."

The riding school ponies neighed in agreement.

"*Pah!*" shouted Divine. "Fools, all of you! This isn't over yet. It's just the beginning." She reared up, her cloak billowing behind her, and galloped across the beach to the cliff path.

Chapter 7

Pippa led Snowdrop onto the beach. Hawthorn and Bramble were splashing in the surf. Hawthorn had sand all over his legs and seaweed hanging from his tail.

"I love splashing," he whinnied. "Come and play with us, Pippa."

"Don't be silly," said Rose. "We haven't got time to play."

"Oooh, silly, are we? At least we're

not prickly like you, Rose, or should we call you *Thorn*?" snorted Bramble.

"I'd love to play, but we have to get back to the castle," Pippa interrupted. "Queen Moonshine and King Firestar are waiting for us. Aren't they, Stardust?"

"A castle!" said Petunia. "With a real king and queen? I need to practice my curtsy first." She trotted away on her own and began to curtsy to an imaginary audience.

"Line up, everyone," said Stardust. "Pippa and I will show you the way to my home. Hop on my back, Pippa."

"Pippa's my girl. She can ride me," said Snowdrop, coming to stand on Pippa's other side.

Pippa blushed. She didn't want the ponies to argue over her. She ran her hand down Snowdrop's neck. "It's probably better if I ride Stardust, here in Chevalia. It's a long way back to the castle and there are some dangerous trails. I'd hate it if you fell and got hurt."

Disappointment flashed in Snowdrop's eyes. She blew softly through her nose at Pippa.

"You're the perfect girl, always putting the pony first."

Pippa and Stardust led the riding school ponies up the cliff path. They stopped for a rest at the top, and then Stardust started back to Stableside Castle at a gallop. Pippa hunched over Stardust's neck with her hands wrapped in her mane. The wind made her eyes water, but she loved the sense of flying and urged Stardust to gallop faster. They arrived in the castle courtyard in a clatter of hooves. Royal Ponies rushed from every corner of the castle to greet them.

"Are these the riding school ponies?" asked Queen Moonshine. "How charming."

"I'm sure I'm really a princess. I think I was switched as a foal," said Petunia. She stepped forward and curtsied to the queen and king.

Queen Moonshine hid a smile as she graciously bowed her head.

"Welcome to Stableside Castle. I'm sorry your first impression of the island was so frightening. You're safe from Divine now, and better still, you're free from the humans who have mistreated you. I trust you will all be very happy, living here in Chevalia."

"Live here?" The riding school ponies turned to each other in alarm.

"But I want to go home," said Rose.

"Me too," said Sunflower. "I can't wait for Billy to ride me in the competition."

"Harry's riding me," said Bramble. "We're going to win the sack race."

"Jess and I have spent hours practicing for the dressage," wailed Rose. "I can't let her down now."

Snowdrop stepped forward and curtsied. "Your Majesties, Chevalia is a wonderful place, but our home is special too. We love working with all the girls and boys who visit us. Some come back every week, and we've made lots of friends. We never asked to be taken to Chevalia. Our home is with the children at the riding school."

"I see," said the queen. "Then home

you must go. But will you stay for the surprise birthday party we are having for our youngest foal, Stardust?"

"Definitely! I never say no to a party," said Snowdrop.

"A royal party," beamed Petunia. "My kind of party."

Stardust's smile was brighter than a candle. "Come on up to my room, everyone, and I'll lend you some things to wear. Snowdrop, you'd look great in my second-best tiara, and Hawthorn, you'll love splashing in my bath with my gorgeous Mane Street Salon strawberry-scented bubble bath. Pippa, all your clothes are here from our last adventure."

A short while later, Pippa, wearing a daisy-print dress and sparkly sandals, and Stardust, in her best pink diamond tiara, led the riding school ponies into the courtyard. The girl ponies were neatly groomed and wore tiaras on their heads, and the boys had brightly colored sashes around their necks. Everyone's hooves glimmered with gold paint, and Petunia's hooves were painted with pink and silver–striped hoof polish.

"Look at the courtyard," breathed Stardust. "I love the glitter balls."

"The ribbons are pretty too, and the flowers," said Pippa.

A pony quartet sang to everyone from the stage. Pippa loved dancing, and to her amazement so did Snowdrop.

"You've got great rhythm," she shouted over the music.

"Mrs. Woods taught us to do dressage to music," Snowdrop said modestly.

After the dancing there was a banquet. Pippa ate her favorite food of chicken fingers and fries, washed down with lemonade. The Stableside cook served it personally to her on a plate with a knife and fork and a glass. There was ice cream with strawberries to follow. The ponies ate honeyed oats, sugar-dusted carrots, and barley-dipped apples. There was a huge birthday cake in the shape of a golden horseshoe and topped with candles.

"*Happy birthday, dear Stardust, happy birthday to you* . . ." Pippa sang heartily, and she clapped the loudest as Stardust

blew out all her candles in one breath. "Wish," called Pippa. "Don't forget to make a wish."

Stardust gave Pippa a secretive smile. "It already came true," she said.

Pippa felt a warm glow inside her. If she had a wish, it would be to return to Chevalia to have more adventures with her princess pony friend. But Pippa knew it was almost time to go back to her world.

Cloud had been enjoying the party from the air, but now she swooped lower. "It's time to go home, Pippa."

Pippa said her good-byes and then climbed onto Stardust's back. Cloud and Stardust rubbed noses. There was a crack and a flash of light. Snowdrop jumped back in alarm. "You've got wings!"

"Me too," whinnied Bramble, who'd just rubbed noses with Cloud. He flapped his feathery brown wings in delight. "Human world, here I come!"

A strong wind lifted Pippa's hair as Stardust rose higher into the air. The

riding school ponies wobbled as they flew after them, but soon they were swooping along like giant swallows. Pippa sat back, her hand resting on Stardust's neck, as the pony flew her home. Cloud led them back to Horseshoe Cove. It was exactly as Pippa had left it with the tide still in and the morning sun bright in the sky.

"Are you staying for the competition?" she asked Stardust.

Stardust shook her head. "I'd like to, but I have to get back to my family. I was behaving like a silly foal, thinking that they didn't care about me. Next time something upsets me, I'll know to talk to them about it, instead of galloping away."

"Talking when something upsets you is always a good idea," said Pippa. "Good-bye, Stardust," she said and threw her arms around Stardust's neck and buried her face in her mane. It was soft and silky, and Pippa never wanted to let go. Swallowing back her tears, she said bravely, "See you soon, Stardust."

"It's a promise," Stardust replied.

Pippa slid to the ground. The riding school ponies joined her, their wings disappearing as they landed. When the last pony touched down, Stardust and Cloud flew away. Pippa waved until the sky was empty. She turned to Snowdrop.

"Shall I ride you back to the stables?"

Snowdrop stared silently back. Pippa

touched her tiara. It was cold. Now she was safe and didn't need to get to Chevalia, the magic was sleeping. She looked into Snowdrop's eyes. They seemed to be saying, *yes please*.

Pippa placed her hands on Snowdrop's neck and jumped onto her back. "Come on, ponies. It's time to go home."

Chapter 8

As Pippa rode into Barley Field Stables, Mrs. Woods ran out of her office.

"Pippa? Oh my goodness, look at you." Her mouth opened in surprise as she helped Pippa dismount. "What . . . where . . . I don't understand . . ." Mrs. Woods moved along the line of horses, touching each one on the neck as if to check that it was real. "Brave Snow-drop, prickly Rose, princess Petunia, sunny Sunflower, bumbling Bramble, and Hawthorn—you've got seaweed in your tail. Where have you all been?"

Pippa took a deep breath. She knew she should never lie to adults. "They were magically shrunken by a mean pony and taken to a special island called Chevalia."

But of course Mrs. Woods didn't believe her. "Oh, Pippa, you have such an active imagination! The important thing is that they're back!"

Mrs. Woods pulled her cell phone out of her pocket. "I'll have to call the parents and tell them the competition is on again. I'd better call the police and let them know the ponies are safe too. This is marvelous news. Thank you, Pippa."

"It was nothing." Pippa smiled as she

went to the tack room to get Snow-drop's grooming kit.

Pippa brushed Snowdrop until her arms ached. She braided her mane and tail and then she oiled her hooves. "You look perfect," she said, standing back to admire her handiwork. Snowdrop stared back and Pippa knew from the jaunty way that she held her head that the pony thought so too!

The competition was a huge success. Bramble and his boy, Harry, won the sack race, and Sunflower and Billy won the egg and spoon. Rose and her rider, Jess, won the "Chase Me Charlie," a jumping contest where the jump keeps getting higher. Petunia and a little girl named Florence won "Best Turned Out." Pippa had to bite her lip to stop herself from giggling as Petunia trotted past, carrying herself like a proper princess pony.

To Pippa's delight she and Snowdrop won the jumping contest. The spectators gasped then clapped loudly as the pair sailed over the wall together. Afterward, Pippa and Snowdrop cantered around the ring in a lap of honor, showing off their big blue ribbon. When they'd finished, Mom, Miranda, and Jack came over.

"You were marvelous," said Mom. "What a lovely end to the vacation. You can pin the ribbon on your bedroom wall when we're back in Burlington Terrace."

Pippa dismounted and gave Snowdrop a big hug.

"Thank you for being wonderful and brave," she whispered.

"Isn't Snowdrop adorable?" said Mom. "Wouldn't it be marvelous if we could just shrink her, so you could pop her in your pocket and take her home?"

Pippa smiled at Snowdrop. "I think Snowdrop's very happy, right here."

Chevalia Now!

EXCLUSIVE INTERVIEW WITH PRINCESS STARDUST

by Tulip Inkhoof

I caught up with Princess Stardust at her dazzling birthday ball, following her amazing adventure in the human world.

☆ **TI (Tulip Inkhoof):** I've always dreamed of going to the human world. Is it true that all the humans can talk there?

☆ **PS (Princess Stardust):** Oh yes, Tulip! Their world is very funny because the humans talk, but the ponies don't. Well, not unless someone from Chevalia is around. Our magic lets the ponies talk. It's amazing!

☆ **TI:** What kind of adventures did you have when you got there?

☆ **PS:** Pippa's bedroom wasn't big enough for me so she took me to the riding stables! Although they were filthy and unsuitable for a princess pony, the ponies boarding there were very nice, just not accustomed to royalty. So I trotted out

2

into the field to sleep under the stars, and that's when something terrible happened.

☆ **TI:** Oh no! Tell us more.

☆ **PS:** Divine followed me to the human world, and then she magically shrunk the stable ponies and took them back to Chevalia.

☆ **TI:** How frightening!

☆ **PS:** Yes, but Pippa and I returned to Chevalia to find the missing ponies!

☆ **TI:** Stardust, you've truly become one of the bravest ponies on Chevalia.

☆ **PS:** Not *the* bravest?

☆ **TI:** Okay, *the* bravest. Happy birthday, Stardust!

3

Chevalia Now!

is delighted to reproduce this special letter from Pippa, received via Princess Stardust.

Dear Stardust,

I'm writing to you from the backseat of my mom's car. We're driving home to Burlington Terrace, and I can't believe our vacation is over. Snowdrop and I did really well in the competition. Mom was so proud of me, and Miranda even gave me a high five, which is just like a medal coming from her. Even my little brother, Jack, said he wants to ride ponies now. I am really looking forward to coming back next year! Mom says we can. I can't wait to spend time at Barley Field Stables and ride Snowdrop, but what I want more than anything is to see you again.

Will I ever return to Chevalia? It's such a magical place, and I'm going to miss it so much. Sometimes at night I dream of galloping in the Fields, or jumping over fallen branches in the Wild Forest.

School starts very soon and I don't know if anyone will believe the adventures we've had. I hope you know that you can always come to me if you ever need help again. I'll keep my tiara close, just in case.

Your best friend,
Pippa MacDonald

P.S. I'm going to put this letter in a bottle and throw it into the river. I just know it will float out to the sea and find its way to Chevalia.

Don't miss Pippa's journey to find the golden horseshoes and save Chevalia!